Mission

a novella

E. J. Myers

Mission

a novella

E. J. Myers

Montemayor Press
Montpelier, Vermont

for my brothers,
Dan and Rick

Mission

a novella

E. J. Myers

W e come in peace."
So they said, and this claim appeared to be accurate. They had perpetrated no violence of any kind. No bombs, bullets, or projectiles. No poison gas or biotoxins. No shock waves, no death rays. No warships—pods, saucers, landers, or marauding tripods. The new arrivals presented no aggressive postures, no threats, no hostile motions. Indeed, they went about their business in the most benign manner imaginable. They were often evident but never menacing, much less destructive. Far better than the alternatives, surely. Even so, the situation wasn't without its downside.

"Here they come again," Mari said, standing near the front window and peering out over the lawn.

Derek left the kitchen table, crossed the room, and stood near the sink to gaze outside.

Two of them were coming up the walkway. Always two. Always a man and a woman—or, more accurately, a "man" and a "woman." Always well dressed, though in the least interesting attire. The "man" in a polo shirt, khaki slacks, and baseball cap; the "woman" in an off-white skirt, floral blouse, and comfortable shoes. They looked as if they'd just finished breakfast at Denny's or had begun their rounds after the Outreach Committee's weekly meeting at a nearby church. If they'd been human, their appearance would have suggested a sixty-ish couple, but their slow, determined gait up the walkway hinted at much greater age. Or not. There was no way of knowing. By now they were reaching the front porch.

Derek pulled away from the window just as he heard the doorbell.

1

"What should we *do?*" Mari asked.

"Nothing! Don't answer!"

He felt dismay—dread—when she opened the door.

"Hello!" said a cheery male voice around the corner. "And how are you this lovely morning?"

"Fine," Mari told them, "but we're not interested."

"We'll take just a quick moment," said a female voice.

As opposed to a *slow* moment? Derek asked himself. Is that the time you have up there in your cosmic neck of the woods? By then he had left the kitchen, walked over to the front door, and stood beside Mari.

"Sorry," Mari said. "This just isn't a convenient time."

"What we have to tell you is important," the male announced cheerily. "Indeed, it's the most important thing you'll ever know. We're here to share the delightful and uplifting—"

Derek swung the door shut fast enough to make his point but not so quickly as to slam it. At once he bolted the lock.

"Was that a good idea?" Mari's face showed more discomfort that he would have expected.

"What would you suggest?" he asked. "This is the third time they've stopped by in just a week. We've got to make the point. Who knows where this is heading?"

"Isn't that the point? If we treat them courteously, there's less risk. If we're rude or insulting, who knows what happens next?"

"There's been no blowback."

"*Blow*back!"

"You know what I mean."

"The question is what *they* mean."

Which was true. No one knew the answer.

Walking the short distance to the living room windows, Derek and Mari watched the couple as they proceeded down the walkway at their slo-mo pace, turned, and moseyed (if that was the right word) up the sidewalk. Nothing about them suggested annoyance or humiliation, much less anger. If anything, they looked entirely content, talking and gesturing, by all appearances at ease with the brief interaction and with whatever else their tour of the neighborhood might bring.

"Looks like they'll go visit the Sandersons," Mari said.

"Good luck with *that!*" Derek replied with a laugh. "If Mel won't even tolerate the neighbor kids walking on his lawn, he'll be *thrilled* when alien life forms drop by to chat."

Later, once the couple had clearly left the area, Derek stepped out onto the porch and found what he was expecting: a leaflet tucked between the mailbox and the brick wall. He pulled it free and took it inside.

Learn All About Zog!

Zog was, in fact, the core issue. *Zog!* Was this some kind of joke? Apparently not. By all appearances these creatures possessed a complex, sophisticated civilization; they had employed incomprehensibly advanced technology to cross intergalactic space; they had arrived on earth without initial detection; yet they worshipped a god named Zog. Couldn't they do better than that? Despite all their capacities and accomplishments, they seemed to have no more imagination than a 1950's-era grade-B sci-fi script writer.

Who was Zog, then, and who were these aliens who had gone to great effort to alert humans to his (or her, or its) importance? Nobody knew.

Various TV shows tried to answer the question, of course, and special reports offered all manner of speculations. Some of these programs focused on scientific aspects of the situation: panels of experts discussing the issues. Where these humanoids came from, how they got here. Aspects of their biology. Summaries of recent incidents from around the world. Conjecture about the future. Derek found it almost impossible to find a cable news station that didn't feature its latest take on the situation. Meanwhile, the Web buzzed with rumors, worries, and outlandish theories. Nobody knew much about the new arrivals, so people of manifold backgrounds tossed the same few facts back and forth.

More common over the past few weeks were discussions of the aliens' so-called mission. They had clearly arrived on earth to promulgate their religion. This mission appeared to be the sole reason for the new arrivals' coming to Earth. ("Mission" was the humans' term, not the aliens'.) What was this religion? What were its beliefs? What were its terms, so to speak, its requirements and consequences? Who was Zog, exactly? How should humans respond to the offer that these new arrivals—Missionaries, as they were soon nicknamed—now presented? And so forth. The various mainstream stations explored the terrain of these issues as gingerly as soldiers scanning a minefield with metal detectors. The standard scenario involved a panel discussion. A talk-show host or news anchor interviewed three or four members of the clergy. The typical array included a minister, a priest, a rabbi, and an imam. The exchanges were (as the introductions for these programs always stated) "wide-ranging and open-minded." The pastors all came off as remarkably tolerant and restrained. A typical statement: *The truth is, we still don't know much about their message.* Or: *Actions speak louder than words, and their actions are peaceable.* Or: *It's important for us all to keep listening to what they say.* Predictably, sectarian cable stations took a less ecumenical approach. More than a few evangelical programs featured clergy who labeled the Missionaries "the devil's minions," "fallen angels," or "spawn of the anti-Christ." Several Catholic priests denounced them as "an affront to Christ's Gospel." At least one rabbi noted that nothing in the Bible, the Talmud, and the other Jewish holy books left much space, if any, for affirming what these Missionaries claimed about Zog. Derek heard roundabout from Hindu and Buddhist colleagues at work that their own clergy, while less judgmental about the mission, weren't exactly thrilled with its message.

There had been *incidents.* The early demonstrations—crowds in Dallas, Colorado Springs, Memphis, Salt Lake City—drew lots of attention at the time but soon faded in comparison to what followed. Protests erupted worldwide. Most but not all had played out peacefully. Little time passed, however, before the protesters routinely ran amok. The upheavals in Moscow,

Jakarta, Oklahoma City, Charleston, and Delhi were especially appalling. Christian fundamentalists marched, picketed, and sometimes physically assaulted the Missionaries they encountered. Devout Muslims in Iraq, Egypt, Indonesia, and Somalia rioted, and, in more than a few incidents, attacked the new arrivals. Just as reprehensible were the many smaller but more numerous and often violent outbursts. Even non-religious groups across the globe—gangs by any other name—had lashed out against the Missionaries with harassment, beatings, and attempted murders. Remarkably, no aliens had died in these attacks. The absence of deaths was less a matter of good luck than a situation that clarified with each succeeding attack: these creatures couldn't be killed. Stabbings, hackings, and gunshots did no harm. Some people conjectured that the 100% failure rate might slow or eliminate these assaults: the humans committing them would soon grasp their pointlessness. On the contrary, the aliens' ability to survive enraged the attackers and triggered more assaults. What was this resistance to mortal injury, some of them asked, but a further sign of the invaders' diabolical nature? They were evil incarnate. Yet Derek, among countless other people, noted that these murderous efforts had no discernible effects on the aliens' *attitudes*. They remained placid, cordial, altogether unaffected by the violence visited upon them. Their response to even the most vicious attacks resembled how a polite human might respond if accidentally bumped while walking through a supermarket aisle: "Oh! So sorry!"

Most remarkable, most bizarre, most bewildering was the so-called BREC incident. This involved a group in the Middle East calling itself the Brotherhood to Re-establish the Caliphate. Derek had read various news reports about what happened—they were unavoidable—and had discussed the situation with friends and strangers alike. He was aware, like everyone, of the notorious video clip. He had always felt an aversion to viewing horrible events of the kinds that so many people now found acceptable, even entertaining. Car wrecks, plane crashes, natural disasters, gang attacks, murders . . . Since when had watching people suffer awful deaths become an acceptable pastime? The very notion was repulsive, obscene. This particular incident, especially: an execution! Yet Derek proceeded anyway, having heard that he couldn't, *shouldn't* skip it, no way, what happened was just unbelievable, he'd never guess the outcome in a million years. Reluctantly, he went ahead. He clicked on the link and braced himself.

The scene: a desert landscape. The *dramatis personae:* fifteen or twenty BREC jihadis. The men sport caftans and turbans. A few wear ski masks. Most stand clutching AK-47's. Two of them lead their prisoner into an open area. Men crowd around in clusters. At once Derek saw that the captive is a Missionary— clearly "male," wearing the usual business-casual attire and smiling the usual smarmy grin. He doesn't appear at all upset. He goes along with his captors as if joining a church picnic. The men leading him stop abruptly. A hooded jihadi facing his comrades raises a huge knife as though stabbing the sky. Someone else reads from a paper. The Missionary kneels. Then the executioner grabs the prisoner's hair, tilts his head, and saws through the exposed neck. The effort looks easy, no more strenuous than cutting through a big marshmallow. There is no blood. Decapitated, the body falls to one side. The executioner holds up the head for all to see. Then, after just a moment, he and the others notice that the head is still talking. The body, too, continues gesticulating where it lies on the sand. The executioner drops the head and backs away. Some of his comrades retreat, too, while others step forward to get a better look. They watch with the same astonishment that Derek, too, felt as while viewing the video. The head soon grows a body, a process that resembles a beach toy inflating. The body lying nearby grows a head. When the two regenerated Missionaries force themselves up and dust off their bodies—one fully clothed, the other naked—the crowd backs off further. One of the jihadis, gutsier than the rest, steps forth with his assault rifle and guns down the humanoids, their bodies blowing apart into fragments as white and irregular as shards of Styrofoam. The jihadis step closer to confirm the destruction of their enemies. Yet a bizarre sight meets their gaze. Each piece regenerates into another being—ten of them, fifteen, twenty, no, an entire a platoon of Missionaries—twenty-five or more. Males and females alike, all naked, all "anatomically correct," as many commentators noted later. They look not the least upset about finding themselves so abruptly in the desert. Less so, certainly, than the jihadis, who, glancing at one another, turn all at once and flee like startled deer.

Derek felt relieved when a full week passed without anyone ringing the doorbell. Some kind of tension lingered in his flesh and bones, however, much as when, during a long series of migraines many years ago, he used to wonder when the next twinge would announce impending agony. Fortunately, he somehow earned a reprieve.

The situation at work was more problematic. As the Patient Advocate at the local medical center, Derek monitored and responded to concerns and complaints among the hospital's inpatients. This role kept him busy under the best of circumstances. A scattering of patients on any given day presented their grievances. Derek headed up the team assigned to resolve disputes, ease frustrations, calm anxieties, and cool tempers. He liked his work, respected his colleagues, and enjoyed helping people. Lately, however, a new kind of problem had started cropping up with surprising frequency. This past week, no fewer than four people had complained about *them*. In one case, a woman believed that her roommate was an alien. Why? For no plausible reason. The complainant herself had a history of clinical paranoia, most likely the cause of her delusion. Two days later, a man flew into a rage when a fellow patient asked if he believed in God. The interlocutor was an evangelical, not an alien Missionary, but the first patient's sense of intrusion resembled what an inquiry about Zog might have prompted. Two other, similar incidents occurred toward the end of the week.

In short, Derek wasn't the only person on edge. On the plus side, Mari's work at the med center's ICU seemed to have spared her similar frustrations. She did, however, overhear patients or patients' relatives discussing the Missionaries' arrival in this or that neighborhood. Both Derek and Mari felt relieved that the medical center itself had been spared any visits.

"So here's what I did," Alex told the gathering of Derek and Mari's friends during the backyard barbecue that weekend. "Maybe I shouldn't have, but I did." Alex, a physician in the cardiology department, made his confession: "I set up a spy cam in our downstairs bathroom."

"You're kidding," said Elena, one of Derek's colleagues on the med center's Quality Management team.

"Dead serious. I know it sounds pervy, but I went ahead anyway. Margie knew about the plan, too—she was fine with it. Weren't you?" He turned to his wife.

"Totally," Margie said. "More than fine—I helped him install it."

"Remind me never to use your bathroom!" Mari exclaimed.

"Believe me, we'd never do anything like this otherwise!" Alex stated, gesturing earnestly. "Ever! And of course we turn on the camera only when Missionaries show up. Tell me honestly: aren't *you* wondering? Who *are* they? Are they what they seem to be? What do they look like in, you know, *private?* Are they equipped like humans?"

The other people present all looked uneasy, curious, or both.

Alex continued: "What do they do when we're not looking? Sneaking a peek might be worthwhile. Maybe that humanoid exterior is just a façade. If so, what's underneath? Could be anything. I can imagine viewing video footage and seeing one of 'em go into the bathroom, lock the door, then pull off his human mask to reveal a drooling reptile face."

Nervous laughter rippled through the group.

"Or, who knows, maybe he'll expose robotic sensory devices

instead of eyes, nose, and mouth. Or he'll retain his outward appearance, but he'll untuck his shirt, extract a power cord from his navel, plug it into the 110 socket, and recharge his battery."

Alicia, one of Mari's fellow ICU nurses, interrupted: "Cut to the chase! What happened?"

"You're gonna kill me."

"If you don't finish your story," Derek told him, gesturing with the big barbecue fork as he stood near the grill, "I'll probably do just that."

"Nothing happened! The guy just walked in, stood for a moment at the mirror, then combed his hair, washed his hands, and polished his glasses with a Kleenex. He leaned closer to the mirror and grinned, checking to see if his teeth needed brushing. Seriously! Then he smoothed his shirt, turned, opened the door, and walked out."

Derek couldn't stop thinking about the BREC incident. To see one of the Missionaries decapitated was bad enough. To see him *regenerate!* That should have felt reassuring but didn't. It was, instead, appalling. To see the two new aliens gunned literally to pieces and then spring forth as twenty-five or more of the same creatures: how unbearably weird. So weird that many people had no recourse but to turn the weirdness into a joke. A snarky Millennial somewhere out there in cyberspace had even made a remix video now viral on the Web—the BREC execution set to Paul Dukas's "The Sorcerer's Apprentice." Instead of Mickey Mouse watching broomsticks proliferate à la *Fantasia*, however, Missionaries multiplied somewhere in the Syrian desert.

An unnerving memory surfaced without warning. Ninth-grade biology class . . . The teacher, Mr. Beasley, instructed the students how to cut up planarians, also known as flatworms. The lesson wasn't a dissection as such but, rather, a demonstration of how these primitive creatures could replicate. Sliced in half, a single flatworm develops into two complete organisms. Sliced into ten pieces, the planarian becomes ten new flatworms. Sliced into as many as two hundred seventy-nine slivers, each two-hundred-seventy-ninth of a worm regenerates into a complete creature. Pondering this memory, Derek recalled the mix of fascination and disgust he felt when, as a fourteen-year-old, he had followed Mr. Beasley's instructions, mutilated several of these little beasts, and produced an entire vibrant menagerie. How different, then, were the Missionaries?

N ot *again*."
   Ringing just one day later, the doorbell hit Derek like a splash of cold water.

Mari, finished eating dinner by now but still sipping her wine, turned toward the living room, then gazed back at her husband.

"Ignore them," he said. "This is just so thoughtless! It's *suppertime*, damn it! These creatures may not bother with food up there, but we stupid earthlings like a little sustenance now and then."

"I'll tell them we're busy." She scooted her chair backwards.

"Don't."

She stayed seated.

They stared at each other for a moment; then Derek went back to eating.

The doorbell again!

Derek said, "We can't let them get the wrong idea. Even shooing them away shows we're willing to interact."

His dismay curdled into annoyance when Mari got up, walked around to the foyer, and opened the door. Though telling himself to stay seated, Derek stood and followed her anyway.

"Hello there!" said the woman beyond the screen.

At once the man beside her said, "A very good evening to you both!"

"It was good till you interrupted our dinner," Derek said, speaking from where he stood behind Mari.

These comments did nothing to wipe the grins off their faces. "We do apologize!" the woman announced. "We're aware that there's no convenient time in our busy world."

"*Our* busy world, actually."

"*Honey*," Mari said.

"Yes indeed!" exclaimed the man. "Your busy, busy world. Which is why we ask just a moment of your time."

"We don't have a moment," Derek said.

"It won't take long, we promise."

"This isn't convenient," Mari interjected. "We have work to do even though we're home now."

"We do understand," the woman stated. "There just aren't enough hours in the day, truly!" He laughed a fakey laugh— *Ha ha ha!*—like a middle-school kid in the class play. "Unless, of course, you learn all about Zog. Then there's all the time in the world. Indeed, in the universe."

"We're still not interested," Derek told them.

"Once you learn about Zog, you'll be interested. We guarantee it. So interested you'll wonder why you wouldn't speak with us earlier."

"Some other time," Mari said.

"No other time," Derek said firmly. "Sorry to be rude, but we're done. Have a good evening." With those words he backed off, waited for Mari to step away, too, and closed the door.

He couldn't believe it when she abruptly pulled the door open again.

"Actually," Mari told the Missionaries, "maybe now's okay."

Under his breath Derek asked, "What are you *doing?*"

His surprise turned to dismay when she opened the outer door, too, and said, "Please come in."

The couple stepped into the foyer. The man removed his cap—the perfect gentleman!—and held it at his side. The woman clutched her white purse demurely. He wore gray slacks and a blue blazer, she a sage green velour pantsuit. Her pale brown hair clung to her head as if in a 1950's-era coiffeur, and his nearly bald pale sported a stringy comb-over.

When Derek glanced disapprovingly at Mari, she avoided looking back.

"Won't you join us?" she asked. Mari then led the guests into the living room and gestured toward the sofa.

Derek hesitated. He wouldn't participate. He would just go sit in the kitchen. He followed the others anyway. Despite his annoyance—his anger, even—he felt too curious to hold back.

Everyone sat.

"My name is Mari," she told them. "And yours?"

The man said, "Herbert."

Staring for a second, Derek fought the urge to snicker. "Herbert," he said. "You come here from across the galaxy and your name is *Herbert?*"

"Indeed it is."

"What's your real name?"

"I have two names. One is Herbert, the other is known only to Zog."

"Why am I not surprised."

Mari spoke fast enough to interrupt him. "And yours?" she asked the woman.

"Agnes."

"I've always liked that name."

"No doubt Zog does, too," Derek noted.

Once again his wife intruded. "May I offer you something to drink? Water? Soda? A glass of wine? Beer?"

"Thank you kindly," said Agnes, "but that's not necessary."

Derek said, "Fun, though, perhaps? Booze—one of us earthlings' best inventions. Well worth traveling a thousand light-years to sample."

"No thank you," said Agnes.

"A bite to eat, then? We have some nice lasagna."

Herbert smiled his grinny grin grin. "That's most thoughtful of you, but we're not hungry. Zog eases all hunger."

Derek tried a different tack. "Let me get this straight. You don't eat. You don't drink. What do you guys do for *fun?*"

"Fun?" asked Agnes.

"Amusement. Entertainment. Good times."

"We contemplate Zog," said Herbert.

"Quite a laugh riot, surely."

"Zog is everything we need."

"Folks," Derek said, "let's set aside Zog for just a moment."

A look of puzzlement came over the Missionaries' faces. "Set aside?" Agnes asked. "What else is there but Zog? What else that matters?"

"Good question, but that's something we'll get to later."

"Zog isn't later. He's always *now.*"

"Then he's present, right, and won't mind a brief detour."

"Detour?

Derek grew impatient. "What do you guys *do* up there? What's your planet like? What do you see around you?"

Agnes, pausing for a moment and looking pensive, said, "Ah, yes—what we see. The most splendid sights. Ours is indeed the most beautiful planet. You must realize, however: all planets are the most beautiful, for all are the handiwork of Zog. Your planet, too, is the most beautiful, the most splendid. Just like ours."

"What my husband is wondering," Mari said in a conciliatory tone, "is—could you be a little more specific?"

"Which means?"

"Could you provide some detail? Is it watery or dry? Is it flat, hilly, or mountainous? Do you have cities full of people, or do you live spread out across the land?"

Herbert said, "We live in the lovely place bestowed upon us by Zog."

16

"That's not specific," Derek said.

"It is the *truth*. Since truth is the very nature of Zog, what I tell you is everything we need to know."

"Maybe for *you*," Derek said, "but I still can't visualize any aspect, any feature, of what you're describing. I'm totally in the dark."

Bafflement came over his expression. "It is daytime now."

Mari said, "He's using a figure of speech. A metaphor."

"Met of four?" asked Agnes. "Four of what?"

Derek couldn't restrain himself. "Look—you're not telling us the little things that clarify the situation. You're telling me the big things that give us only a general idea."

"There is only one idea," Herbert said.

"Let me guess: Zog."

Now they both smiled the fullest smiles that Derek had ever seen on the Missionaries' faces.

He couldn't take this any longer. "It's been a long day," Derek said. "We have stuff to do before bedtime. We have to get up early. So—" and now he stood—"we need to wind down our little chat."

"Oh," said Agnes.

Herbert, clearly confused, gave a long look at his companion and turned once more to Derek and Mari. "Well, then."

Standing abruptly, Derek felt annoyed when his wife made no move to leave the sofa.

"Yes," Mari said at last, standing, "We've taken too much of your time."

Agnes protested: "Not at all." She stood, however, and Herbert stood, too, a few moments later.

What a relief when Derek succeeded in shepherding the visitors out of the living room, through the foyer, and onto the porch.

"Thanks for your patience," Mari said.

"It's been a pleasure speaking with you," Herbert said.

"We wish you a pleasant evening," Agnes said.

"Goodbye," Derek said.

The Missionaries descended the front steps.

Before Derek could shut the front door, he saw Agnes turn and climb the steps again. "A token of our appreciation," she said, reaching into her white handbag. She offered a pamphlet to Mari, who, as Derek watched with dismay, accepted it.

Unity with Zog!
Unity with Zog's Creation!
Unity with Those You Love!
Both Present and Departed!

He knew at once that everything had changed. Knew even though Mari said nothing else about the Missionaries as they walked back inside. Knew precisely because she said nothing. Knew even though Mari set the pamphlet on the foyer table as if indifferent to its presence. Knew because she placed it right next to Sari's photo on the tabletop, like an offering.

The overall situation appeared to ease. Few incidents occurred over the next few days. Parties hostile to the Missionaries seemed to start grasping that further attacks would serve no purpose. If earthlings could only refrain from killing the aliens, their number wouldn't increase. The most recent reports suggested a worldwide population of perhaps three thousand. Left alone, the Missionaries went peaceably about their business. They were a distraction and a nuisance, not a threat.

It's true that some fanatics of the human persuasion now tried turning the tables. That is, people attempted to out-mission the Missionaries. Catholics, Evangelicals, and Mormons preached to the new arrivals; members of certain Muslim sects proselytized to the extra-planetary infidels; and partisans of less-prevalent faiths made comparable efforts. The outreach did not go well. Since the aliens had no need for food, drink, sleep, or sex—indeed, no need for *anything*—the spiritual debates over tenets and doctrines left the human religionists struggling to maintain their stamina when confronting the Missionaries' inexhaustible patience, relentless good cheer, and appetite for interminable discussion. Even the most ardent proponents of earthly religions soon grew weary, diminished their efforts, and, increasingly, just gave up.

This situation didn't mean that the aliens weren't present. Derek noticed at least a few of them each day. Driving to the medical center, he noticed one couple making their rounds in a nearby neighborhood. Buying groceries after work, he spotted another pair handing out leaflets in front of the local Safeway. Sitting in a coffee shop one afternoon, he caught sight of another pair chatting with passersby on the sidewalk. He read in the local paper that some of the Missionaries now lived in the area: had rented apartments. A few had sought employment. Doing *what?* he wondered. Mostly low-paying, menial work. Stocking supermarket shelves. Emptying trash cans for the municipal sanitation department. Working as flaggers on road crews. Derek found it surprising that anyone would offer them jobs, but some of the news reports clarified the situation. "I wasn't crazy about hiring him," one shop owner stated, "but I took a chance anyway. And you know what? He's been great. He shows up on time, he does what I ask, he's careful and hard-working, he's always happy, and he never complains. Tell me this: where's the problem? I don't give a darn where he's from—and I'd hire a dozen more like him if I could." Which, predictably, gave rise to complaints that these aliens were taking jobs that rightfully belonged to earthlings. But most people, Derek included, felt that these developments suggested less trouble, not more.

Yet a worrisome incident took place at the medical center. The Quality Management team learned late one afternoon that a local EMT squad had transported one of the Missionaries to the Emergency Department. The victim, Randall by name, had suffered an accident. Specifically, he had stepped off the curb without noticing a car backing up at that moment, which resulted in the vehicle's right-rear tire crushing his left foot. The head E.D. physician paged Derek and alerted him to the situation. Quality Management would need to know the big picture. Derek interrupted his rounds among the hospital's in-patients and rushed downstairs.

The entire Emergency Department staff was visibly tense. Nurses, doctors, and technicians pretended to go about their business while clearly monitoring one particular examination room. Two med center security guards flanked the doorway.

Once cleared to enter, Derek found the injured Missionary, two doctors, and two nurses inside. The patient, attired in a blue-and-white hospital johnny, chatted affably with the staff. He looked younger than Herbert, with a full head of sandy brown hair and a smoother complexion. His left foot, smashed into a disc as flat as unbaked bread dough, protruded from the sheet and blanket laid over him on the gurney. The head E.D. physician, Dr. Urvesh Patel, looked up, nodded, then stepped away from the bedside and accompanied Derek out into the hallway.

"So," said Derek.

"Indeed," said Dr. Patel.

"And?"

"All rather bizarre but under control. As you surely noticed, this gentleman has suffered a severe crushing injury, yet his discomfort is minimal, and he appears almost complacent about his condition."

"Is he at risk of dying?"

"Not that we can determine. Compared to most patients in the same state, he seems scarcely affected."

"Is he cooperative?" Derek asked.

"Altogether."

"How's your staff doing?"

"People are understandably keyed up but perform well in their customary roles."

"Is there a plan? Surgery, perhaps?"

Chuckling, Dr. Patel said, "Surgery! That's what's most remarkable. All this fellow wants is hot water."

"I'm not sure I understand," Derek told him.

Dr. Patel explained how Randall had informed the staff of a simple resolution to his problem: if he could soak his foot in water heated to one hundred twenty degrees Celsius, the crushed appendage would repair itself. "Hot water initiates the healing process," Randall had told the doctors and nurses present. "Zog takes care of the rest." There was a problem, however. Dr. Patel informed the patient that at sea level on Earth, water boils at one hundred degrees Celsius. No matter how much heat you apply at this altitude, the temperature of water won't get any a hotter. Randall then asked an appropriate question: "What if we increase the pressure?" The E.D. staffers discussed the option with the patient. One of the physicians present, Dr. Katerina Blacic, Chief Medical Officer for the medical center, stated, "There's the hyperbaric chamber." Dr. Patel now explained to Derek that the medical center's resources included a room used for treating certain conditions—gangrene, anaerobic infections, carbon monoxide poisoning, and others. The components of this room allow the option of increasing the ambient barometric pressure to help treat such conditions. So, yes, there was a plan.

Derek listened to this explanation feeling both astonished and relieved. Not an easy situation but capable of resolution. The last thing the medical center needed was a maimed or dead Missionary. "Who would've thought we'd ever face something like this," he said as they finished their discussion.

"Obviously we'll need to mobilize the Ethics Board immediately," Dr. Patel said. "Unorthodox procedures on non-human patients! Not ideal!"

"The folks at Billing will be thrilled," Derek noted. "Imagine the turn-around time for invoices sent to a galaxy far, far away."

Later, Derek learned from Katerina that the entire process went without a hitch. Urvesh, two other E.D. staff doctors, and two nurses transported Randall to the hyperbaric chamber; they set him up for the procedure; they essentially boiled his foot in a container of water heated to a hundred twenty degrees Celsius; and, within a few minutes, the Missionary's ruined appendage reshaped itself into a normal-looking, fully functional foot. The doctors and nurses examined the patient and found him altogether healed.

"When I congratulated him on a successful recovery," said Katerina, "he told me, 'I deserve no congratulations. I thank you for your gracious assistance, but I give all other credit to Zog.'"

Only with great difficulty did they persuade Randall to remain in the ICU a day or two for observation.

erek was surprised but relieved when the crisis resolved without further difficulties. He wasn't so sure about the situation at home. Among other things, Randall's transfer to the ICU meant that Mari would know all about this incident.

"How did it go up there?" he asked her as they settled in after work.

"You know I can't tell you, given the HIPAA regulations," she said.

Was she joking? Or just playing hard-to-get? "HIPAA regs don't apply to non-human patients."

"You know we still shouldn't discuss our cases."

He couldn't believe she'd play the stickler. "And you know we fudge the rules anyway. At least a little. Sometimes."

"Okay, you win," she said. "It's not as if you won't find out anyway, given what you do there. So yeah, it went fine. I didn't take care of him myself, but everyone on the unit knew what was happening, and I talked with Beth and Jodie afterwards."

"And?"

"The guy was cured. Completely healed."

"Cooperative?"

"Of course. These people are nice."

"Whatever else, they're *nice*."

"You make it sound like a character flaw."

"It's not a flaw, but it makes me suspicious."

They fixed supper in silence and ate without speaking. Derek tried to raise other topics of conversation but without success. More than once he felt tempted to press the point about Randall the Missionary, but he resisted the urge. Why pour gasoline on the flames?

"They visited him," she said at some point.

"Excuse me?"

"Herbert and Agnes."

"Visited Randall?"

"Of course—while he was in the ICU. They showed up and spent time there. I wasn't assigned to Randall, but I told Alyssa I'd already met Agnes and Herbert, so she put me in charge of looking after his friends when they weren't actually in the isolation room."

"And?"

"What do you mean—*and?*"

"What was it like?"

"What it's always like. They were polite and friendly. They were concerned about Randall, of course, but totally cooperative with the staff and appreciative about what we were doing."

"And pushy about Zog?"

"We didn't talk about Zog."

"Now *that's* a switch."

"Could you ease up a little?" she asked, clearly annoyed.

"Not till *they* do."

"Well, they *did* ease up—they didn't even mention Zog—and that's all I have to say about it."

Derek could tell, however, that Mari had more on her mind than she revealed. Was more curious about the Missionaries than she ought to be. Right after Agnes and Herbert's visit two nights earlier, Derek had felt initially relieved that she hadn't read the new pamphlet. Perhaps he overestimated her interest. At some point during the night, however, he had noticed Mari's absence from their bed—unusual for a sound sleeper like his wife—an absence that circumstantially explained the pamphlet's altered position on the foyer table in the morning.

For this and other reasons, Derek had returned to the foyer when Mari took her shower after breakfast. He had opened the pamphlet and read its contents.

Do you miss those you love? Do you long for your loved-ones – including those now departed from the earthly sphere? Fear not! When you learn All About Zog, you will regain those you have lost to Space, Time, and Dissolution. How? By acquiring the knowledge inherent in Zog.

What do you have to lose? Don't hesitate!

Learn All About Zog!

* * *

He wasn't surprised when, well after dinner, as both of them caught up on paperwork, Mari said, "I don't know how much more evidence you need."

"Evidence," Derek told her.

"Evidence that these people are remarkable."

"Remarkable as a bunch of accountants."

"Don't be so negative! *Hello?* Aliens arrive from deep space. They have no needs—none!—which even you seem willing to admit. Shot or cut to pieces, they can't be killed. Severely injured, they heal themselves by soaking in hot water. Doesn't this stuff make you even the least bit curious?"

"Of course I'm curious," he said. "I just want to hear about something other than Zog."

"What if that's the key?"

"The key to what? The most boring god in the universe?"

"You don't know he's boring."

"No? He's the Velveeta of supreme beings."

"Give me a break," she said, her annoyance morphing into anger.

"I'm trying to. But you know what? I'm concerned. Concerned you're getting snookered." He knew where this was going. He felt a gravitational pull neither of them could resist. Better, then, to jump instead of falling. "Nothing will bring her back," Derek told her. "Nothing will undo what happened. Sorry to be blunt, but I'm telling you the truth. Neither heaven nor unity with Zog will give you what you're longing for."

He wasn't surprised when Mari stood and left the room.

Twins were like clones, he noted, still seated in the living room. *Were* clones. The cloning hadn't occurred in a creepy sci-fi way, much less by the even creepier means of an alien getting decapitated. All the same, one life had become two. Mari's embryo—or perhaps Sari's, or perhaps the proto-Mari/Sari's—had split apart a few days after conception, had developed in utero as two side-by-side embryos, had emerged as two genetically and outwardly identical baby girls. This much Derek had learned from Mari, who, early in their relationship, never tired of explaining how she and her sister had entered the world. He had also heard countless stories about Mari's and Sari's early years. How they were inseparable from the start. How they grew rapidly and thrived in all respects. How they formed an alliance from babyhood onward that united them in all ways at all times. How they delighted, reveled, and rejoiced in their closeness. How they dazzled everyone—their parents, their extended family, their family's friends, even total strangers—with their beauty, intelligence, and charm. How they relished their ability to confuse everyone outside the family as to which of them was which . . . and indeed, how they confused even their own parents at times, a confusion that allowed for all manner of mischief and pranks when they played switcheroo games at everyone else's expense. How, proceeding through their school years, they drew constant attention for being both individually remarkable yet essentially indistinguishable. How, when they reached their teens, they drew yet more attention as they blossomed from pretty girls into gorgeous young women. How they stayed close even upon graduating from high school, left for college—attending the same school, of course—and entered their respective romantic relationships and early careers. How they both acquired degrees in highly technical areas of nursing. How they chose to share an apartment despite their boyfriends' objections. How the intensity, depth, and seeming indestructibility of this sororal bond continued as if forever until it didn't—until, as it so happened, Sari died in a car accident at the age of twenty-seven.

Now, almost twenty years later, the situation was— *What was it?* Derek had experienced enough grief to know that the experience wasn't as simple or brief as most Americans wanted it to be. There was no tidy "closure" at a certain point. The feelings of loss diminished over time, it's true, but they ebbed and flowed anyway, sometimes welling up suddenly and forcefully. He himself still missed his father, dead now for more than a decade. He felt the ache of longing for friends who had suffered fatal illnesses. He knew he couldn't begin to imagine what Mari felt even twenty years after Sari's accident. To lose someone who was genetically the same yet an altogether different person . . . To lose the sister who had been a lifelong pal, soul mate, confidant, best friend, ally, refuge, and co-conspirator . . . To lose the person who was both Self and Other.

"Don't judge me," Mari said later, as they got ready for bed.

"I'm not judging you," Derek stated, his voice louder than he intended.

"You're watching me and thinking what you're thinking."

"I'm just standing here."

"You're standing there and thinking, *Mari's off the deep end. Mari's getting hoodwinked by these wacko aliens.*"

"That's not true and not fair. I'm just concerned. I'm not convinced this Zog business will be helpful."

He knew she would exclaim, *Zog business!* but instead she told him, "Look—you'll never get this. You can't get this. Sari and I were the same person, only different. We were different people but only one. When she died I died, too, only I didn't. I'm still here. Nothing can prevent me from wanting my other half back."

"But nothing will ever make that possible."

"We don't know that, do we?"

News reports revealed that a certain number of people were taking the bait. They were, in their own words, "learning all about Zog." What did that mean, exactly? Even after watching the most comprehensive programs, whether online or on TV, and after reading accounts in newspapers and magazines, Derek couldn't tell. Was there some kind of training? An initiation? A mystical experience, perhaps? Nobody could answer these questions. Even detailed interviews with humans who learned *all about Zog* offered no clarity. The respondents seemed as vague as the Missionaries. Derek could determine only that these people were diverse in geographical origin, ethnicity, gender, social class, and so forth. The Missionaries offered equal-opportunity suckerhood.

Derek sat in a med center conference room with two of the hospital chaplains, Father Javier Osorio and Rabbi Jan Ehrlich. "So, here's the setup for a joke," Derek told them as they settled in with their coffee and pastries. "A priest, a rabbi, and a space alien walk into a bar . . . " He fell silent, waiting for their reactions.

"That won't get you very far," Javier said. "These aliens don't drink."

"Point taken," Derek said.

"Maybe teetotaling is your punch line," Jan said.

They bantered for a while, then settled in to discuss the med center's overall situation. Since both the Quality Management team and the Pastoral Care providers focused on aspects of patients' emotional wellbeing, Derek often interacted with the various chaplains. He had worked for many years with Javier and Jan; he respected them; he felt close to them. Hanging out today—just chatting, not conferring more officially—always felt like a treat. For twenty or thirty minutes they compared notes on various issues, told stories about recent interactions, and speculated about upcoming issues. Notable were aspects of the Missionaries' presence in the community. Many patients seemed agitated about rumors of aliens lurking somewhere in the hospital. In addition, congregants at Javier's church and at Jan's synagogue had voiced anxieties about what the extraterrestrials might do in the future. Neither Derek nor the chaplains knew how to respond.

"What kinds of concerns are your people expressing?" Derek asked them.

"Oh, little things," said Javier, "such as the arrival of the Antichrist, the start of the Tribulation, and the imminent end of the world."

"How about yours?" he asked Jan.

"Genocide," she said.

"That's kind of far-fetched, isn't it?" Derek asked. "I mean, given how peaceable these Missionaries seem?"

She made a quizzical gesture. "Maybe so, but let's just say that we Jews know a thing or two about genocide. One of them is that 'peaceable' can be the thin edge of the wedge."

"Fair enough." They sat in silence for a while. Then Derek said, "Have the Catholic or Jewish authorities commented about what's happening behind the scenes? Has there been any kind of outreach? Any dialogue, for lack of a better word?"

"Judaism has no hierarchy," Jan said, "hence no central authority figures who could reach out to the Missionaries. That being said, various Jewish organizations have interacted with them in one way or another. A delegation of rabbis went to ask questions. Tried to get a sense of what they're about."

Javier listened to her comments, then laughed abruptly. "Meanwhile, the Catholic Church is nothing if not hierarchical!

To an almost military degree! So yeah—the Vatican sent a squadron of cardinals to meet with the Missionaries."

Derek waited for one of them to follow through. "And?" he asked, sounding even more impatient than he felt.

Javier and Jan exchanged glances, each apparently wanting the other to speak first.

Jan shrugged quizzically. "The delegation of rabbis agreed that the interactions were all rather vague."

Javier said, "Ditto for the cardinals. Nothing much happened. I heard through my order that the meeting went well— was respectful, even cordial, but incredibly— Incredibly what? *Inconclusive.* The cardinals came away with little or nothing you could call information."

"No clarity about goals?" Derek asked. "Beliefs, even?"

"Not really. Just what we already know. The Missionaries have what we would call a religion, their god is Zog, and they want to share their knowledge of this god—him, her, it, whoever—with us poor benighted humans. They offer this knowledge to one and all. End of story."

"So it seems."

For a long time they just sat there. Derek started to find the silence uncomfortable. "Meantime, there's a personal twist on the situation. My wife seems rather intrigued."

"By the Missionaries?" Javier asked.

"By the Missionaries."

"Really!" Jan exclaimed.

"Specifically, she's intrigued and moved by their promise of union with the deceased—with departed loved ones. Twenty years ago Mari lost her identical twin in a car wreck, so she's longing not only for the beloved sister but also for her other self, if that's the right way to put it. Apparently that's often a big issue for twins."

Both chaplains waited, listening attentively.

"As you can imagine, the notion of regaining what's been lost is . . . *compelling.*"

"I would imagine so," Jan said.

Derek said, "The fact that these people can regenerate adds fuel to the fire. Especially in the mind of someone with a deceased twin."

"Does she somehow believe," Javier asked, "that these Missionaries can offer—can confer on others—what they seem able to accomplish for themselves?"

"Quite possibly."

"What do the Missionaries have to say on that point?"

"That's the big question, isn't it? One they haven't really answered. Not to me, anyway."

"To Mari?" Jan asked.

"Unclear." After a pause he said, "Or if it's clear to Mari, it's not a clarity she's willing to share with me." He paused again. Interesting, how these chaplains, like psychotherapists or police interrogators, could keep you talking just by falling silent. "As you can imagine, that's causing some marital tension."

"I'm sure that's very difficult," Javier said.

"Quite," Derek said. Although hesitant to ask for counsel, he went ahead: "Any suggestions?"

Jan shrugged in a way that somehow conveyed support rather than dismissal or indifference. "This is a tough one. Suggestions? I wish I had some. Just that Mari's a big girl and can make her own choices."

"Rightly so. But that doesn't exactly ease my concerns," Derek said.

Driving home after work, he found himself awash in thoughts, feelings, and recollections. Mari was brooding about Sari; now Derek was, too. Twenty years had passed since the accident. Derek knew that even two decades couldn't heal such a profound loss. He and Mari had spoken frequently about her twin. He knew his wife thought about Sari all the time. Fair enough. Now the memories came bubbling up for him as well.

He and Sari had been close. No surprise there: if he felt delight, admiration, and affection for Mari, why wouldn't he feel warmly toward someone virtually identical to his wife? Both sisters were intelligent, generous, caring, funny, and beautiful. Both shared many interests with Derek, including their careers in the health care professions. From the start of his relationship with Mari, her twin had been supportive and open toward Derek. He knew he was lucky to have such a strong bond with his sister-in-law, especially given what he'd learned about past issues when one or another of these women had resented a romantic partner's arrival on the scene and resulting changes to the sororal bond. But this situation created its own issues. Derek felt uncomfortable at times about how much he liked Sari and how much the liking seemed mutual. Pleased, too, of course . . . but also uneasy. Feeling the love, delight, and desire he felt for Mari, why shouldn't he feel something similar for the woman who was, in Mari's own words, both the same and other? Early on, especially, Derek sometimes lost track of which sister was which. He might walk into the kitchen and carry on several minutes of conversation with Mari as they prepared dinner before grasping that the woman next to him wasn't Mari at all but, in fact, Sari. He simply hadn't paid close enough attention to the subtle, miniscule, often almost imperceptible differences that distinguished one sister from the other. During these early phases of the relationship, too, the twins still enjoyed playing the occasional prank at others' expense. Switcheroos were, if nothing else, a way of teasing their respective partners into paying closer attention to them. Did they also indulge in this mischief just for fun? No doubt. That wasn't clear. The question itself prompted both puzzlement and fantasies. If the twins had switched places and, pulling off the ultimate prank, had sent Sari to bed with Derek, would he have known? Would he have grasped that the woman in his arms wasn't his wife? The question both unsettled and aroused him. He had always felt intense lust for Mari. Why not feel the same desire for Sari?

G ood evening!" said Agnes late that afternoon. Derek, having poured himself a scotch and soda on arriving home, was puttering in the front yard when the couple ambled up the walkway. "Sorry, can't talk."

"We come in peace," said Herbert.

"Fine. Now go in peace." He'd been trimming the front hedge. Holding a pair of long-bladed clippers, Derek felt the sudden impulse to attack them. A single snap of the blades would shear off each head. But why bother? Four Missionaries would soon stand before him, each smiling and yammering about Zog.

"We've come to speak with your lovely wife," Agnes said.

"My lovely wife is at work and won't be home till later."

"We talked with her at the hospital," Herbert said. "She invited us to stop by."

"Fine, but she's not here."

"When will she return?" Agnes asked.

"Like I said, not till later. Much, much later. To be honest, there's no telling when, exactly, given what can happen on an evening shift." He decided to switch the subject: "How's your buddy Randall?"

"Doing splendidly well, thank you," said Herbert. "So unfortunate, that little accident. And, speaking frankly, an embarrassment to all of us visitors! We don't want to cause any problems! But I have to tell you: Randall has received excellent attention at your medical facility. Absolutely first rate."

"You sound surprised."

Herbert laughed nervously—*heh heh*—and said, "One never knows in this day and age."

"Meaning, we earthlings are generally incompetent?"

"Not at all!" Another laugh. "You are a splendid species! Technologically quite advanced! Often compassionate! We were all impressed by the level of genuine concern."

Agnes said, "The only point of awkwardness was that people asked Randall a lot of questions. So many people. So many questions. But everyone was *nice*. Now Randall seems likely to leave the hospital this evening."

Derek couldn't restrain himself. "Good. Give him my regards. Meanwhile, Mari's not home. She won't be home for hours. Even once she's here again she'll have her hands full."

"We'll come back later."

"Don't come back later. Don't come back at all." He set the shears on the porch. Best to avoid the risk of impulsive actions.

"She told us to," Agnes said.

"There was a misunderstanding."

"There was no misunderstanding," Herbert said. "She made it clear she wants to speak with us."

Startling himself as much as Herbert, Derek reached out abruptly with both hands, grabbed the guy's lapels, and twisted them around his fists so hard that he winched his victim forward. Their faces nearly touched. Herbert's expression showed surprise but nothing that resembled fear. "Listen to me," Derek said. "You're going to leave and never, ever come back. Stay away from my wife. If you ever show up again—you two or any of you people—I'll make sure you regret it. I'm not sure how, but I guarantee it. You understand?"

Herbert stared back, blinking just once. Derek had no idea what he saw in those pale blue eyes. The two of them stood so close that Derek could smell Herbert's breath, a cheap floral scent like some kind of dish detergent—Dawn, perhaps, or Palmolive. He felt a twinge of nausea. It occurred to him that Herbert's mouth would now exhale nerve gas, his eyes would emit a blinding glare, or his tongue would protrude as a strangulating tentacle. Who knows, maybe all three at once. Herbert only smiled that door-to-door salesman's smile. "You must be a very sad person," Herbert said. "You have good reason to be sad. I hope that some day, somehow, you move beyond your sadness. We have the means to help you do that, but you don't seem interested. That's the saddest thing of all. Now please unhand me."

Derek released him with a shove. "Get off my property."

Smoothing his blazer, Herbert turned to Agnes, who stood watching nearby but showing no signs of alarm or distress. "We must be going," he told her.

They proceeded down the walkway without looking back.

Derek couldn't believe what he'd done. The last time Derek had assaulted anyone was, what, thirty-five years ago, during his final year of elementary school. A sixth-grade bully named Judson had been making Derek's life so miserable for so long that during recess one afternoon, Derek had suddenly jumped the outsized jerk, put him in a hammer lock, and threatened to punch him out. That impulsive act had terminated Judson's abuse forever but at the cost of Derek getting suspended for two full days. What might result from roughing up Herbert? Probably nothing. If these Missionaries could tolerate getting beheaded in the desert, surely they wouldn't retaliate for a brief episode of manhandling. Alien-handling! Still: not good. Derek cringed at the thought of his own behavior. Roughing up that extraterrestrial insurance salesman! Even if nothing else came of Derek's perpetrating this assault, Mari—assuming she heard about the incident—would be furious.

Stepping into the house, he stopped short when he saw the sisters' photo on the foyer table. *Good God they're beautiful!*—both of them in the glory of their late twenties. Mari still is, now in the mature beauty of her late forties. The creamy Irish complexion. The lustrous auburn hair. Those eyes . . . deep green in full sunlight, mysterious gray in less intense illumination. The real mystery, though: which of the twins was which? Derek had always assumed that in this photo of two young women standing arm in arm, Mari was on the left, Sari on the right. But maybe not.

He walked into the dining room, pulled up a chair, and sat. What did it mean, he wondered—*You must be a very sad person?* And: *You have good reason to be sad.* By what right could Mr. Comb-over Alien tell Derek what he was or wasn't? He felt sad only when he thought of Mari getting conned by these intergalactic hucksters. Or was that the point? Was she getting conned? Or was she right to keep her mind open? *Doesn't this stuff make you even the least bit curious?* she had asked him. No: just as he had never felt curious when, during his boyhood, he spent summers at the Good News Bible Camp, nor later, in college, when fellow students witnessed to him. None of what they yammered about made him *the least bit curious.* Why, then, or how, did Mari have the capacity to wonder? Maybe her Catholic upbringing—all those nuns at the parochial school— explained it. Or perhaps it was Mari's own response to being *a very sad person* with *good reason to be sad.* Why not, given her loss?

He sat there for a long time. Glanced at his watch: almost nine-thirty. When Mari worked the evening shift, Derek almost always fixed himself a simple supper and ate alone, knowing that she wouldn't be home until midnight. He didn't feel hungry now. He went to the kitchen, poured a glass of wine, returned to the dining room, and sat once again. Stayed there. Waited.

*   *   *

She didn't arrive till nearly one a.m. Walking in, Mari saw him at once and said, "You're still up."

"And?"

She huffed at him. "*And!* What a nice way to greet me."

"Did they find you?"

Her initial expression of surprise now morphed into annoyance. "Let me at least put down my things." She walked to the kitchen with her purse, took a detour to the bathroom, and returned. "Why are you upset?"

"Herbert and Agnes stopped by again."

"So I hear."

"They told you what happened?"

"They said you were—impolite."

"Something like that," he said. Then, after hesitation: "So now what?"

"Is this a deposition?"

"I just want to know what happens next. Do you get beamed up to the mother ship? Teleported across the Milky Way?"

Mari gazed at him with a completely unfamiliar expression. Not anger. Not contempt. Not dismissal. Some kind of *difference,* some kind of different-ness. Some kind of Mari-ness that Derek didn't recognize. A chilling thought occurred to him: what if the woman standing before him wasn't Mari, but Sari? What if the accident twenty years ago had killed his wife, not his sister-in-law? What if Sari had switched places with her twin to spare Derek the pain of loss? Had interposed herself in his life, his house, his bedroom, his bed, as a kind of changeling? What if he had spent the past twenty years living with someone other than the woman he had married? No, that was ridiculous. All of it. Yet as he gazed at Mari now, Derek understood that he didn't know who she was. Had no idea.

She said, "Look—I'm tired. You're tired. We're not getting anywhere. Let's just call it a day."

"Maybe so."

Neither of them got up. Derek reached across the tabletop and rested his hand on Mari's forearm, less to offer consolation than to take hold of her, though he knew she was already gone.

About the Author

Born in Denver and raised in Colorado, Mexico, and Peru, E. J. Myers attended Grinnell College and the University of Denver. He has worked in a wide variety of professions and trades, including inpatient health care, emergency medical services, carpentry, cabinetmaking, and publishing. He is the author of forty published books, most issued by mainstream companies, among them four novels (*The Mountain Made of Light, Fire and Ice, The Summit,* and *Last Things*); fourteen children's books; and a well-received, much-reprinted book about bereavement, *When Parents Die: A Guide for Adults.* He has also co-authored or ghostwritten over a dozen books for clients or other authors. He lives with his wife in central Vermont.

For information about E. J. Myers, visit his Web site at:

www.edwardmyerswriter.net

About Montemayor Press

Montemayor Press is an independent publisher of litera-
ture for adults and children. To learn more about our books,
visit:

www.MontemayorPress.com

or write for a catalogue at:

Montemayor Press
P. O. Box 546
Montpelier, VT 05601

Books by E· J· Myers
Available from
Montemayor Press

Fiction

Fever - 978-1-932727-17-3
Last Things - 978-1-932727-24-1

The Mountain Trilogy

> *The Mountain Made of Light* - 978-1-932727-04-3
> *Fire and Ice* - 978-1-932727-04-3
> *The Summit* - 978-1-932727-04-3

Nonfiction

Lovely, Dark and Deep - 978-1-932727-26-5
Pond Meadow Moon - 978-1-932727-29-6
The Whiteness of the Weasel - 978-1-932727-31-9

Books for Young Readers

The Adventures of Forri the Baker - 978-0-9674477-0-4
Climb or Die - 978-1-932727-12-8
Duck and Cover - 978-0-9674477-8-X
Ice - 978-0-9674477-9-8
Solos en la Montaña - 978-1-932727-18-0
Survival of the Fittest - 978-0-9674477-2-8

www.ingramcontent.com/pod-product-compliance
Lightning Source LLC
Chambersburg PA
CBHW071217130626
46555CB00004B/1743